Karen's New Holiday

Little Sister

Karen's New Holiday
Ann M. Martin

Illustrations by Susan Crocca Tang

A
LITTLE APPLE
PAPERBACK

SCHOLASTIC INC.
New York Toronto London Auckland Sydney
Mexico City New Delhi Hong Kong

The author gratefully acknowledges
Helen Perelman
for her help
with this book.

ISBN 0-590-52376-7

12 11 10 9 8 7 6 5 4 3 2 1   9/9 0 1 2 3 4/0

Printed in the U.S.A.   40
First Scholastic printing, August 1999

Rainbows and Chocolate Stars

"My turn!" I said as I threw my lucky round stone on the ground. I hopped into the first square and picked it up. I, Karen Brewer, am a very good hopscotch player.

It was after dinner, but still light enough for us to play outside. And it was the end of summer, so the days were still long.

Hannie Papadakis took her turn next. Hannie lives across the street and one house down. She is one of my best friends. I have two best friends. But I'll explain that in a minute.

Just as I was about to take my turn, I heard music coming down the street, little bells ringing a familiar tune. It was Mr. Tastee!

"I scream, you scream, we all scream for ice cream!" Hannie and I sang as we jumped up and down. We love ice cream, especially the kind from Mr. Tastee's truck. We ran inside our houses to get money.

"Mr. Tastee is here!" I shouted as I opened the kitchen door.

"All right, Karen," Nannie said. "You do not have to yell." Nannie is always reminding me to use my indoor voice.

"Can I have an ice cream too?" Andrew asked. Andrew is my little brother. He is four going on five. He has blond hair and blue eyes just like me. He loves to do everything I do, so of course he wanted to have ice cream from Mr. Tastee.

Nannie gave us money, and Andrew and I ran outside. Hannie was already in line. Timmy Hsu and his brother, Scott, were paying for their ice cream.

2

"Hello there, Karen!" Mr. Tastee said.

I am a very good customer. That is why Mr. Tastee knows my name.

"What would you like tonight?" he asked. "I have some different cones and pops. Did you notice the new sign on the side of the truck?"

I looked over at the new sign. There were so many ice creams! Hannie and I read all the flavors. So did Andrew. (I taught him to read.) He picked the red spaceship pop. I wasn't sure which one I wanted.

"I am going to have a Rainbow Pop," Hannie said as she looked over the sign.

The Rainbow Pop looked very pretty. But there was a new chocolate cone with chocolate stars on it. Hmmm. It was a tough choice.

"Come on, Karen!" Melody Korman said. She was behind me in line. Melody lives across the street. I guess she already knew which ice cream she wanted.

"I am going to have the new Chocolate Stars cone," I said to Mr. Tastee.

Mr. Tastee smiled and winked as he handed me my ice cream. "Excellent choice, Karen. This is one of my favorites."

"Thanks, Mr. Tastee!" I said.

Hannie, Andrew, Timmy, Scott, Melody, and I sat on the grass in front of my house and ate our ice cream. When it started growing dark, we chased fireflies around the yard. Fireflies are like bugs with little flashbulbs. They are very hard to catch.

"Karen! Andrew!" Elizabeth called from the porch. (Elizabeth is my stepmother.)

Andrew and I said good night to our friends and went inside our big house.

Being a Two-Two

Guess what. Andrew and I have not one but two houses. In fact, I have two of lots of things. And so does Andrew. I will tell you why.

A long time ago, when I was little, Mommy, Daddy, Andrew, and I all lived together in the big house in Stoneybrook, Connecticut. (It is the house Daddy grew up in.) But then Mommy and Daddy started fighting all the time. Soon they decided to get a divorce, and Mommy, Andrew, and I moved to a smaller house in Stoneybrook. (Andrew and I call it the little house.)

I still had my bedroom at the big house with Moosie, my stuffed cat, and all my toys and clothes. At the little house I had another stuffed cat named Goosie (he looks just like Moosie) and other toys and clothes. I even split Tickly, my special blue blanket, in two so I could have it at both houses.

Soon Mommy started dating a man named Seth Engle and they got married. Now Seth is my stepfather. He is a carpenter and builds really nice furniture. He also likes animals. He has a dog named Midgie and a cat named Rocky.

Daddy also got married again, to Elizabeth Thomas. She already had four kids. Charlie and Sam are in high school. Kristy is in eighth grade and is the best big sister ever. David Michael is seven like me. And, after Daddy married Elizabeth, they adopted my little sister, Emily Michelle, from a faraway country called Vietnam. She is two and a half and very cute. I try to be a good big sister to her. I even named my pet rat after her.

Elizabeth's mother came to live in the big house after Emily Michelle was adopted. Nannie helps take care of everyone and everything. She has started her own chocolate business. She works in the new addition off our kitchen. (It always smells good in there.) Her chocolates are yummy!

Lots of pets live in the big house too. David Michael has a Bernese mountain dog puppy named Shannon. And we have a black kitten named Pumpkin. Then there are our fish. Andrew's is called Goldfishie and mine is called Crystal Light the Second. David Michael takes care of them for us when Andrew and I are at the little house. Plus, Andrew has a hermit crab, and I have my rat. They go back and forth between the big house and the little house with Andrew and me.

Andrew and I get to spend lots of time with both our mommy and our daddy. We switch houses every month. We spend one month at the big house, then one month at the little house. That means I get to be near one of my two best friends no matter where I am. Nancy Dawes lives next door to the little house. And Hannie lives near the big house. We call ourselves the Three Musketeers. We even have a motto. It is "All for one and one for all."

I have two mommies, two daddies, two cats, and two dogs. I have two stuffed cats and two bicycles, one at each house. I have two sets of toys and books and clothes. I have two best friends. I even have two pairs of glasses! (The blue ones are for reading and the pink ones are for the rest of the time.) That is why I made up special names for Andrew and me. I call us Andrew Two-Two and Karen Two-Two. (I thought up those names after my teacher read a book to our class once. It was called *Jacob Two-Two Meets the Hooded Fang*.)

You may think being a two-two is hard. But really it makes everything two times more fun.

Shopping

After breakfast the next morning I sat at the kitchen table, reading a brand-new chapter book.

I had just finished a chapter when Nannie asked, "Karen, would you like to go to the store with me?"

"Yes!" I cried as I jumped up from the table. Nannie frowned at me. "I mean, yes," I said again, with my quiet indoor voice.

"Good," she said. "I have to go to the Paper House. And I could use your help."

(Ever since Nannie started her chocolate

business, she is always running to the store for something.) Nannie said Mr. Morgan (he owns the Paper House) had an order ready for her. Nannie buys little white boxes from Mr. Morgan's store to put her chocolates in.

I got into Nannie's car and buckled my seat belt. Nannie drives a pink Cadillac. Charlie calls it the Pink Clinker. It is old and very big. I love to ride in the car with Nannie.

When we got to town, we walked along the street and I looked at all the store windows. The first store was a hardware store. Its window was not very exciting. A few hammers and screwdrivers were hanging on a boring blue board. The next store was a clothing store with lots of fuzzy sweaters and long pants in the window. Nobody would wear those clothes in the summer! Where were the bathing suits and shorts?

The Paper House was the third store. In the large window I could see lunch boxes, apples, rulers, crayons, and pencils piled in front of a long blackboard. Someone had written BACK-TO-SCHOOL SUPPLIES on the blackboard. What was going on? It was August, not September!

"Nannie," I said. "Why does this window have back-to-school things in it?"

Nannie looked at the window. "Well, lots of times stores start putting up back-to-school window decorations in August."

"Why?" I asked. "There's no school in August."

"No, there is not," Nannie agreed. "But stores like to decorate their windows for the holidays. And since there are no holidays in August, like the Fourth of July or Christmas, some stores decorate the windows for back to school instead."

That didn't seem right. I could think of plenty of decorations for August. Where were the pails and shovels? The ice-cream cones? The watermelons? There had to be holidays in August for showing off summer decorations.

I asked Mr. Morgan about his window display.

"We always need window displays. People buy more things when they see a nice display," he said. "I know school does not start for awhile, but there are no holidays in August so we always make a back-to-school display."

No holidays in August? I couldn't believe it. August was the best and happiest month. How could there be no holidays?

I helped Nannie carry the bags to the car. I wanted to get home quickly. I had to check the calendar right away.

Calendar Check

When Nannie and I returned home, I ran into the kitchen. Kristy was sitting at the table helping Emily Michelle color.

"Hi, Karen," Kristy said. "Do you want to color with us?"

"My flower," Emily said as she held up her drawing.

"That is a beautiful flower," I told her.

Usually I love to color with Kristy and Emily. But I had to find a calendar.

I looked on the refrigerator. All of the boxes on the calendar were written in.

When ten people live in a house, a calendar can fill up pretty quickly. There was so much written on the days, it was hard to see any holidays.

"Karen, what are you doing?" Kristy asked.

I told her about the windows and what Mr. Morgan had said.

"We could check your dad's calendar. It is on the desk in his office," Kristy said. "Let's go see."

I followed Kristy into Daddy's office. His calendar was lying open on his desk. It was a big brown leather book with a different page for every day. Kristy explained that holidays were written in red ink in the page corners. We looked carefully at all the days in August.

"Look," I said, pointing to August second. I had already found a page with tiny red letters in the corner.

"August second was Friendship Day!" I said. "I wish I had celebrated that day with Hannie and Nancy. That would have been a great thing to do with the Three Musketeers."

"You can celebrate next year," Kristy said as she flipped through the calendar.

"And look, Susan B. Anthony Day," I read. "Who is she?"

"She was a very important woman," Kristy said. "She did a lot for our country. She fought for women to have the right to vote in elections. There is even a coin with her face on it."

Well, Susan B. Anthony Day wasn't like a holiday, when you get presents or you get to dress up. Mr. Morgan could not make window displays for his store for that.

"I'm sorry, Karen," Kristy said. "It looks like Mr. Morgan was right. There are no big holidays in August at all."

Kristy went back into the kitchen to finish coloring with Emily Michelle. I sat down in Daddy's chair and stared at the calendar. There are thirty-one days in August. But no big holidays were listed.

August was one of my favorite months, and there was no day to celebrate. Boo and bullfrogs.

Kid Power!

It was raining when I woke up the next morning. For once, the big house was very quiet.

Andrew and I played Nintendo for awhile. We raced each other in the Real Race Chase game. I picked the Princess driver and he was the Turbo Man. I won, but I let David Michael play Andrew next. I was getting a little bored. I decided to see what everyone else was doing on this rainy day.

Charlie was at the movies with his friends, and Sam was on his paper route.

Kristy was baby-sitting, and Emily Michelle was taking a nap. Nannie and Elizabeth were busy with a big chocolate order, and Daddy was working in his study. How boring.

I read my new chapter book for awhile, and then I decided to watch my favorite television show, *I Love Lucy*. (Lucy and her best friend, Ethel, are so funny. I always laugh when I watch that show.)

After *I Love Lucy* was over, a TV announcer said, "Stay tuned for *Kid Power!* Kids who make a difference! Meet the kids from Farmington, Connecticut, who used Kid Power to help clean up a park in their neighborhood."

That sounded good. And Farmington was in Connecticut. Just like Stoneybrook. I decided to tape the show for Nancy and Hannie. I did not want them to miss it.

The announcer was a young girl named Julie. She was in Farmington to interview the kids who had organized the cleanup.

"Our friends formed groups called committees," a boy named Stephen Andrews said. "And that way we were able to make a difference in our community."

"What did the committees do?" Julie asked.

Stephen spoke into the microphone again. "Each group was responsible for a different part of the day. One group organized the cleanup schedule, one group collected trash bags, and another group made fliers advertising our big cleanup."

A girl named Alison spoke next. "It was really cool to be a part of this project and help out. I hope that now more kids across the nation are going to get involved in their own neighborhood cleanup."

The camera focused again on Julie. "More than just making their neighborhood park a beautiful place," Julie said, "these kids have sparked a campaign to clean up city parks throughout the country." Julie explained how the kids from Farmington were reaching out to kids across America. Then she finished by saying, "They not only made a difference in their community, but they will make a difference nationally with Kid Power."

Suddenly I had one of my gigundoly excellent ideas! A nationally gigundoly great idea!

6

A Gigundoly Great Idea!

I called Nancy and Hannie and invited them to come over right away. I could not wait to tell them about my gigundoly great idea.

Hannie arrived first because she lives just next door. I took her coat and umbrella. I did not want to tell her my news until Nancy was with us. Finally the doorbell rang. The Three Musketeers were all together.

I told my friends about *Kid Power!* They had not seen the show so we watched the tape. I was smiling when the show ended.

"Karen, what are you so happy about?" Hannie asked.

"Well," I said, "we could —"

"Karen," Hannie interrupted. "We do not have a park that needs to be cleaned up."

"Well, no," I said, "but there is something else we can do."

Nancy looked at me. "What?"

"Mr. Morgan at the Paper House always puts holiday decorations in his store window," I started to say.

"Oh yes, I love that store!" Nancy said. "There are great stickers in the back room."

"I bought a unicorn sticker last week," Hannie said.

"Anyway," I went on a bit loudly, "there are no holidays in August."

"Does he want us to clean up his store?" Nancy asked.

For heaven's sake. "No," I said. "But he needs a holiday for August. We all need an August holiday." Hannie and Nancy still didn't say anything. "We could make a new national holiday with our own Kid Power!" I said.

Nancy and Hannie just stared at me. They were speechless.

Then Hannie said, "What do you mean?"

"I mean," I said, "that we can make a new holiday!"

"And be on television?" Nancy said. "Like the kids in Farmington?" Nancy, like me, wants to be an actress when she grows up.

"Sure!" I said. "We will be the founders of the holiday. Television crews will want to film us."

"The holiday should be really fun," Hannie added.

"A holiday for kids!" I said. I was glad that my friends were excited about my idea.

"We are going to need some help," Nancy said. "Remember, there were lots of kids in the park all working together."

"We can get all the kids on the street to help," I told Nancy and Hannie. "Let's have our first meeting tomorrow morning."

We were going to make history!

Holiday Planners

"All right, we are now starting the meeting," I said. I looked around my backyard. Hannie and Nancy were sitting next to me. Scott and Timmy Hsu were kicking a soccer ball with David Michael, Bill Korman, and Linny Papadakis. Maria Kilbourne was showing Andrew her dog Astrid's new trick. (Maria loves dogs. And Astrid is the mother of David Michael's dog, Shannon.)

"Have you started yet?" Melody Korman said as she ran into the backyard.

"No, you are right on time," I replied.

"Everyone, sit down here in front of me. I will tell you what this is about."

I liked being in charge of the group. I explained about seeing the *Kid Power!* show and how we could make a difference. "We can make a national holiday for August," I said. I opened my new yellow notebook to the first page. It was my official national holiday notebook. "Does anyone have any ideas for the holiday?" I asked. I was all ready to take notes.

"Can there be trick-or-treating on this new holiday?" Andrew asked. "I love getting candy."

"And dressing up," Melody added. "I love wearing costumes."

David Michael stopped tossing the soccer ball in the air. "I think we should get lots of presents, like at Christmas."

"Let's have a parade and lots of food, like on Thanksgiving Day!" Maria said, jumping up and down.

I was having a hard time writing all the ideas down.

"Karen, what about fireworks, like on the

Fourth of July?" Nancy said. "Wouldn't that be great?"

"Yeah, and maybe we could all wear a color, like everyone wears green on St. Patrick's Day," Timmy added.

"It would be cool to stay up till midnight, like on New Year's Eve," Linny suggested.

The meeting was going better than I expected!

"But wait," Bill said. "All these things are from other holidays."

"Yeah," Hannie agreed. "Karen, what will our national holiday celebrate?"

I was not sure. I looked at my two best friends. Just then Nancy's face lit up with a huge smile.

"I know," Nancy said. "We could go to the library and see what has happened in August that we can celebrate."

"That is a great idea!" I said. "We will find out everything about August that we can." I was very proud of my committee. "Let's meet at the library tomorrow."

We were going to use our Kid Power!

At the Library

I took my yellow notebook to the library the next day. I knew that I would have to write down important information.

Our group met outside the library. When everyone was there Kristy and two of her friends took us inside. We walked to the librarian's desk. A woman with long brown hair looked up from her book. A nameplate on her desk said RACHEL BROWN, REFERENCE LIBRARIAN.

"Hello," Ms. Brown said. "May I help you find something?"

"Yes, please," I said in my most grown-up voice. "My name is Karen Brewer, and my friends and I need to find out all we can about August, and about things that happened in August."

"We are making a national holiday," Andrew added. "But we need to find something to celebrate."

"I see," said Ms. Brown with a big smile. "I have a book that might help you."

We followed Ms. Brown to a large round table. She took a fat black book off of the shelf. "This is an almanac," she explained. "It lists all the holidays and festivals in every month of the year."

This was perfect. The almanac was a gigundoly cool book. Ms. Brown went back to her desk, and the committee got to work. I opened the book to August.

"Wow, look at all these," Nancy said.

Lots of festivals and holidays were listed. We crowded around to read the book.

"Hey, National Mustard Day!" Hannie said, giggling.

"Blech," Timmy said. "I hate mustard."

"Look," Melody said as she reached across the book. "There is a National Clown Week!"

The committee was getting lots of ideas. We forgot to use our library voices. Ms. Brown looked up from her book. Kristy told us to settle down. We lowered our voices.

"It says here that the peridot is the birthstone and gladiolus is the flower," David Michael read.

That wasn't anything to celebrate. Boo and bullfrogs.

"There has to be something else!" I said.

Ms. Brown tapped me on the shoulder. "Try to remember to whisper, Karen," she said. Then she sat down at the table with us and turned to another section of the book. "Let me see if I can help you." She turned some more pages and pointed to National Aviation Day. Ms. Brown explained that that was Orville Wright's birthday.

"Who is he?" Scott asked.

"Orville Wright was the first person to fly in an airplane," Ms. Brown told us.

Scott smiled. He loves airplanes. "That is it! We can celebrate flying and dress up like pilots."

"And make cool airplanes," Linny added.

Oh, brother. That was not what I had in mind. "What else is there?" I asked Ms. Brown.

"Well," she said as she flipped through the pages. "August is National Hair-itage month. You can celebrate hair and hair products."

Nancy, Hannie, and I began giggling.

"We could wear wigs," David Michael said as he started to laugh. Then we all started laughing. Melody laughed so hard she snorted. Even Ms. Brown and Kristy started to laugh.

A lady at the next table looked over at us and put her finger to her lips. "Shhh," she scolded.

We tried to stop laughing. It was hard.

But Ms. Brown reminded us we had to be respectful of the other people in the library.

"I hope you find some ideas for your holiday," Ms. Brown said as she stood up from the table.

"Thank you," I replied.

"And good luck with your committee."

I had a feeling we were going to need lots of luck, unless we wanted to celebrate mustard, airplanes, and hair.

"Let's vote tomorrow," I told the committee. "Everyone should come with an idea, and we will take a vote."

Hmm. We had learned about lots of August events, but nothing seemed perfect. Maybe tomorrow we would think of the perfect thing to celebrate.

A Letter to Washington

"**K**aren, would you like some watermelon?" Elizabeth asked. She held out a plate of watermelon wedges. I was sitting outside at the picnic table in the big-house backyard, looking at my national holiday notebook. I was still trying to come up with a good idea for our holiday. Elizabeth sat down with me at the picnic table.

"Thanks," I said as I took one of the wedges. The watermelon was bright red and extra sweet. Yummy!

"What are you working on?" Elizabeth asked, pointing to my notebook.

"My friends and I are going to start a new national holiday for August," I said. Then I told her about *Kid Power!*, Mr. Morgan and the window displays, the calendar on Daddy's desk, and Ms. Brown and the almanac. Elizabeth listened carefully. I told her what a good leader I was for the group. I spit out a few seeds onto the plate and then looked up at Elizabeth. "How do celebrations become national holidays, anyway?" I asked. "I have not really thought about that yet."

"Hmmm." Elizabeth sighed. "I am not sure. But you should start by writing a letter to our congresswoman. That would be the first step."

I turned to a fresh new page in my notebook. "Will you help me write it?" I asked.

"Sure," Elizabeth said. She told me that our congresswoman's name is Jodi Kesser. So I started my letter, "Dear Congresswoman Kesser . . ." But I did not know what to write next.

"Maybe you should first think about all the reasons there should be a national holiday in August," Elizabeth said.

On a separate piece of paper I made a list. This is what I wrote:

1. THERE ARE NO HOLIDAYS FOR KIDS IN AUGUST.
2. EVERYONE LOVES HOLIDAYS.
3. KIDS WOULD NOT HAVE TO MISS SCHOOL BECAUSE THERE IS NO SCHOOL IN AUGUST.
4. PEOPLE LOVE SUMMER!

Elizabeth helped me with some of my spelling (even though I am an excellent speller). I felt very proud about writing a letter to a congresswoman. I told her she could call me to talk more about my holiday idea. She might have questions. After Congresswoman Kesser read my letter, she would bring it to Washington, D.C., and to the Congress . . . maybe even the White House! (I just love Washington, D.C. When I was there with my big-house family we got to see all the famous places.)

I signed the letter with my signature. It looked like this:

Karen Brewer

Then I wrote:

HEAD OF AUGUST NATIONAL HOLIDAY COMMITTEE

under my name. I wanted the congresswoman to know exactly who I was. When I finished my letter, Elizabeth read it over.

"This looks great, Karen," she said. "I will mail it for you tomorrow."

"Thanks," I replied. I could not wait until our committee meeting the next day.

Hooray for August

I love Saturdays at the big house. We always have a huge lunch. Elizabeth calls it a smorgasbord. That means that almost everything in the refrigerator is set out on the table in the kitchen. Everyone makes their own lunch.

I was especially excited this Saturday. Soon my friends and I would vote on our holiday. We did not have much time left in August — only one more week!

I walked into the kitchen. Sam and Charlie were making their famous sandwiches.

They piled on stuff until the sandwiches were almost a mile high.

I made one of my favorite lunches too. It was a peanut butter and banana sandwich. Kristy taught me how to make it.

"I am going to Washington, D.C., again," I exclaimed. Everyone was sitting at the table eating.

"You are not!" David Michael exclaimed.

"Karen," Elizabeth said warningly.

"Well, I might go," I said. "When my national holiday happens."

"What are you talking about?" Sam asked. Only it sounded all muffled because he had just taken a bite of his mile-high sandwich.

"My friends and I are going to make a national holiday for August," I said.

"There are no big holidays in August, and we think there should be one," David Michael added.

"Yeah, a holiday for kids to celebrate!" Andrew said.

I smiled at my brothers. They were good

40

committee members. "We need to find something to celebrate, though," I said.

Sam started laughing. "Maybe you could have a Watermelon Holiday and just eat watermelon all day."

Charlie put his sandwich down. "Or you could have a holiday to celebrate your awesome older brothers. How about that, Karen?" Charlie laughed and slapped Sam a high five.

I did not think they were very funny. Sometimes brothers are not all that helpful.

"All right," Daddy said. "That is enough." He turned to look at Andrew, David Michael, and me. "While some holidays are fun, others, like Veterans Day or Martin Luther King Junior Day, honor important people or events in history."

Daddy was right. I started thinking about the holidays that my family celebrated.

"You and your friends need to think about what is special about August in order to celebrate," Daddy said.

Just then Nannie brought out her new

chocolates. They were shaped like ice-cream cones. The ice cream part was colored sprinkles. They were very pretty. Everyone at the table got one.

As I ate my chocolate ice-cream candy, I thought about what Daddy had said. I thought about the things I loved about August. I ran to get my notebook and wrote down a list of my favorite August activities. I wrote:

1. PLAYING OUTSIDE (EVEN AFTER DINNER)
2. GOING SWIMMING
3. GETTING ICE CREAM FROM MR. TASTEE
4. WATERMELON!

I looked over my list. There was so much to celebrate about August. That was when I realized I wanted to celebrate the whole month — not just one day or event. Hooray for all of August!

Too Many Planners

I waited at the picnic table in the big-house backyard. It was almost time for the committee meeting vote. Nancy and Hannie were sitting next to me, and David Michael and Andrew were throwing a Frisbee. Then Timmy and Scott arrived, and finally Linny, Melody, Bill, and Maria. Everyone was there.

"All right," I said. "We need to vote on our holiday. Does anyone have any ideas?"

Melody stood up. "I went on the Internet with my dad last night and do you know what? Hawaii was made a state in August!"

"Cool," Hannie said.

"I think we should have a luau," Melody's brother, Bill, said.

"We could wear flower leis and grass skirts!" Melody said.

Scott said, "I found out more about Aviation Day. It is a really awesome day with lots of airplane demonstrations."

"It's not like we can do airplane demonstrations, Scott," I said. "We are just a bunch of kids."

"Karen," Hannie said, nudging me. "That was not nice."

"Yeah, Karen," Timmy said. "He was just giving his idea."

I tapped my pencil on the table. "Who else has an idea?"

Maria raised her hand. I called on her.

"My parents always call the end of summer the dog days of summer," Maria said. "So why not celebrate the dogs in the neighborhood?"

Hannie smiled. "That's a great idea!" I

was sure she was thinking about her poodle, Noodle. She loves dogs almost as much as Maria does.

"I think we should have a parade with our dogs," Maria told the committee. "Astrid and Noodle could lead the parade." Maria smiled at Hannie.

"Don't forget Shannon!" David Michael said.

"And Clyde!" Timmy added. Clyde is the Hsus' golden retriever.

"This is supposed to be a *holiday*, not a parade," I said. "Besides, not everyone on the block has a dog."

"It is a fun idea, Karen," Hannie said.

"But dogs do not have anything to do with August," I argued. "My idea is to have a holiday to celebrate August."

Nancy nodded. "Karen is right. But maybe we could have a dog parade on the holiday anyway."

I smiled at Nancy. Then I looked around the table. Everyone seemed to agree. I thought now would be a good time for a

46

vote. "All in favor of our national holiday celebrating the month of August raise your hands!"

Everyone except Maria, Hannie, Timmy, and Scott raised their hands. Seven people for the August celebration and four people against. "August celebration wins!" I cried.

"What are we going to call the holiday?" Andrew asked.

I grinned at my little brother. I had already thought of that. I was about to tell everyone my great idea when Maria jumped up.

"What about Sunshine Day?" she asked.

"It might rain," David Michael said. "Then that would not be a great name."

"How about August Day?" Hannie said.

I could tell the group did not like that idea either.

"Let's call the holiday Augustania!" I blurted out.

Everyone gave a cheer. I knew that I had thought of the perfect name. I looked at

Maria and Hannie. They did not look happy, but they agreed to the idea. Even Timmy and Scott said they would still be on the committee.

We decided that Augustania would be held the next Saturday. That meant we had a lot of work to do.

Elizabeth interrupted our meeting to tell us dinner was ready. Everyone went home. (Nancy ate at Hannie's house.)

"After dinner tonight, everyone meet here," I said. Augustania was really going to happen!

How to Celebrate

After dinner I heard jingling music coming down the street. Mr. Tastee! Andrew, David Michael, and I ran outside. Timmy and Scott were already eating their spaceship pops. And Maria, Melody, and Bill were looking at the sign, deciding what to buy. Nancy and Hannie were almost finished eating their ice creams. As soon as we got in line, Linny came riding down the block on his bike. Our whole committee was there!

Once everyone had bought their ice cream

(I got another Chocolate Stars cone), we sat around the picnic table in the big-house backyard.

"I asked my parents if we could all swim in our pool for Augustania," Melody said. "They said that as long as a grown-up was there, it would be all right."

I said I would ask one of my parents if they would help.

"Let's make sure to have lots of candy on Augustania!" Andrew said.

"Yeah," Linny agreed as he licked his chocolate cone. "And ice cream."

David Michael slurped the last of the red ice off his pop. "We should have a place for make-your-own sundaes!"

"*Yesss!*" everyone shouted.

I wrote down all of the suggestions in my yellow notebook.

"What about presents? Didn't we talk about them before?" Nancy asked.

Everyone agreed that there should be presents on Augustania. I made a note that we should tell our parents about that.

"We can make gifts to give our parents," Nancy said.

"That is a great idea!" I told Nancy. Then I looked around at the group. "Let's make some smaller committees, like the kids in Farmington did."

Everyone seemed to like that idea. Since I am a very good leader, I made a list of things we needed to do. Maria, Linny, Nancy, Hannie, and I wanted to make decorations. Timmy, Bill, and David Michael decided to make plans for the make-your-own sundaes. Andrew, Scott, and Melody said they wanted to work on putting together the Hawaiian luau.

"What about costumes?" Melody asked. "I think we should wear Hawaiian shirts. You know, for Hawaii and the luau."

"What about cool pilot sunglasses?" Scott suggested.

"Why don't we just work on our assignments," I said.

"Karen, just because Augustania was your idea, doesn't mean we have to do everything you say. You should listen to other people's ideas," Hannie said.

Well, boo and bullfrogs. I was listening.

I looked at my committee. There was so much to do. It was hard to make a decision.

I stood up. "Any costume is good on Augustania," I declared. Everyone cheered. "And you should each make one flier of your own for the neighborhood," I said. "Then *everyone* will know about Augustania."

Everyone cheered again. I was good at leading a committee. *Kid Power!* would think so too when they came to interview me.

Spreading the Word

"I wish I could eat that ice-cream cone," I said. I was not standing in front of Mr. Tastee's truck. I was sitting on Hannie's bedroom floor, making fliers for Augustania.

Nancy held up her sign. She had drawn three ice-cream cones and a giant sun on it. The sign said: COME CELEBRATE AUGUSTANIA!

"That looks great," I told Nancy. I looked over at Hannie's sign. She was finishing up a picture of a slice of watermelon. Hmmm, I was getting hungry.

My paper was blank. I did not know what

to draw. Should I draw a swimming pool? Or maybe a pail and shovel? I looked out the window. It was a beautiful sunny day. I could see Daddy's garden. Tons of tall sunflowers were facing up toward the sun. "That is it!" I yelled.

"What?" Hannie and Nancy said together.

"I am going to draw lots of sunflowers," I said. "And I am going to ask Daddy if I can give sunflowers to everyone for Augustania. Sunflowers should be the official flower for our holiday."

My friends thought that was a great idea.

"And yellow should be the official color," Hannie said.

We worked away at our fliers. Kristy had said she would help us put them up on our street. Later, we met Kristy outside of Hannie's house.

"These fliers look terrific!" Kristy said.

The Three Musketeers smiled. We thought they looked good too.

We put the signs up on telephone poles on our street. When we were finished, I

asked Kristy if we could ring people's door-
bells to let them know about Augustania.

"All right. Let's see if Mrs. Porter is
home," Kristy said. Mrs. Porter lives next
door to the big house. I think she might be a
witch. But even Mrs. Porter might want to
celebrate Augustania, so I had to ring the
bell.

"Hello," Mrs. Porter said as she opened
the door. (She was wearing black. Just like a
witch!)

I told her about Augustania. Then I
thought that I should mention the candy to
her.

"Kids will ring the bell," I said. "And they
will say, 'The sun is hot and the sky is blue.
Happy Augustania to you!' "

"It is like trick-or-treating," Nancy added.

I was not sure that Mrs. Porter under-
stood what we meant. But Kristy nudged
my shoulder.

"Thank you, Mrs. Porter," Kristy said, and
the Three Musketeers walked away.

We told a few more of our neighbors

about Augustania. Then Kristy said, "How about a snack?"

I was hungry after seeing those fliers for Augustania. We went back to the big house, and Nannie gave us some watermelon.

Nancy started singing, "Watermelon, watermelon . . ."

"How it drips, how it drips," Hannie sang.

"Up and down my elbows, up and down my elbows," I added.

"Spit out the pits, spit out the pits," the three of us sang.

"Three cheers for Augustania!" I said.

"Hooray! Hooray! Hooray!"

I grinned at my friends. Augustania was going to be the best holiday ever.

Hello, Washington?

After our snack, Hannie and Nancy had to go home. I waited outside with Nancy until her mom picked her up. But even after my friends left, I thought about Augustania.

Then I remembered my letter to Congresswoman Kesser. I wondered if she had brought it down to Washington, D.C., already. Maybe she had talked to the President about my holiday. Since I had not heard from her, I decided to call. Maybe she had some questions about my idea for a new holiday.

I found the big phone book in our hall closet. I looked up the congresswoman's office. I was very excited. I had so much to tell her about Augustania.

"Hello, Congresswoman Kesser's office," a friendly voice said.

"Hello," I answered. "My name is Karen Brewer and I wrote Congresswoman Kesser a letter about a new national holiday." (I used my grown-up voice.)

"The congresswoman is very busy, but she and her staff answer all her mail. You need to be patient," the woman said.

Boo and bullfrogs. Augustania was only a few days away! I hung up the phone. I was not happy. I am not very good at being patient.

"Karen!" Nannie called.

I went into Nannie's kitchen. She was busy tying ribbons on the little white boxes we had gotten from Mr. Morgan. She was filling a large order for the library's summer fund-raiser.

"Would you like to help us?" Nannie asked.

I like to help Nannie. And since I wasn't off to Washington, D.C., to tell the President about Augustania, I had some time to help out. David Michael was cutting ribbon, so I started to tie bows with the ribbons.

As I was tying my third red ribbon on a box, Sam walked in. He was just finishing his paper route.

"Is Shannon going to be in the parade?" Sam asked David Michael.

"Yes," David Michael said. "She'll be the star!"

"What parade?" I asked.

"The Dog Days of Summer Parade," Sam said. "I thought that was part of your Augustania holiday."

I glared at David Michael. "What parade?" I said again.

Sam grabbed a piece of chocolate and popped it into his mouth. "There's a flier

60

down the street with a drawing of a big dog. It says, 'Come celebrate the dog days of summer! Bring your dog to the Dog Days of Summer Parade this Saturday.' "

Well, that was all wrong. I did not know what it was all about. I had to call an emergency committee meeting.

Dog-Gone Mad!

"There has been a big mistake," I said when my friends had gathered in the big-house backyard. I looked at each of them. We were sitting around the big picnic table. "Some people did not follow my directions."

"Your directions were to make our own fliers," Melody said. "And we did."

I stood up and put my hand on my hip. "What did you write on the fliers?"

" 'Come celebrate Augustania! A luau with Hawaiian music,' " Bill said. He smiled at Melody. I guessed that they had made their signs together.

"We made signs for the pie-eating contest," Timmy said, pointing to Scott and Linny.

"A pie-eating contest?" I said. "Pies are for Thanksgiving, not Augustania!"

"Pies are not just for Thanksgiving, Karen," Linny said. "My mom makes pies all the time."

I sat down on the picnic bench and put my head in my hands.

"I thought Maria's signs were really cute," Hannie said.

"Yeah, I'm excited about the dog parade," added David Michael.

But Augustania was not about dogs. I thought I had made that clear. That was not what I had in mind at all!

"My mom even found some Hawaiian music to play at the pool," Melody said.

"And my dad found an old Hawaiian shirt that he is going to let me wear," Bill told everyone.

"Timmy and I got these great aviator sunglasses," Scott said. "We look like real pilots."

I dropped my head on the table and then took a slow, deep breath.

"There are too many different things," I said. "If people do not know how to celebrate Augustania, it will never get to be a national holiday!"

"Karen, we are all working very hard," Nancy said softly.

"Everyone has lots of great ideas," Hannie added.

"But it was my idea!" I said. "Now no one is listening!" I grabbed my notebook and ran inside the house. I did not want to talk to anybody on the committee anymore.

Upstairs in my room, I flopped on my bed. I looked at my calendar and saw AUGUSTANIA written in bright yellow letters. Only three days away . . .

"Oh, Moosie," I said. "What is going to happen to Augustania?"

Moosie is a very good listener. I gave him a big hug.

There was a knock at my door. It was Elizabeth. Since she was not on the committee, I thought that it was all right for her to come in.

"Karen, your friends are all downstairs," she said. "What happened?"

I told Elizabeth that everyone on the committee was a meanie-mo. No one was listening to me, the head of the committee. Augustania was not turning out the way I had thought it would.

"Karen, being the head of something is hard work," Elizabeth said. "You cannot give up so quickly. There is also a lot of hard work involved in making a holiday celebration."

"I have been working very hard," I said.

Elizabeth smiled. "I know you have, Karen. But so has everyone else. As the leader, you need to make some compromises for the good of the group."

"But Augustania was my idea!" I blurted out.

"Maybe at the beginning, Karen. But now you have a group of friends who have helped to make the day very special. A good leader does not only have a good idea, she has leadership qualities. And part of that is making compromises so the job gets done. Every group needs a strong leader."

"Maybe," I said. But I was still mad.

Andrew knocked on the door. "Karen, we are all going to meet tomorrow. We hope you will come."

I looked at Elizabeth. She nodded. Our group needed a leader. Augustania needed me. I would be there.

One Last Meeting

"We all want Augustania to be great, Karen," Nancy said.

My friends were at the picnic table in the big-house backyard again. I could tell that some of them were still mad. I was still mad too. After all, Augustania had been *my* idea. But maybe Elizabeth was right. I should try to work with the other kids. Augustania needed a strong leader.

I opened my Augustania notebook. I flipped to the first page and looked at all our great ideas. Then I turned to my notes from the meeting when we had named Augustania. I had been very proud that day.

"Everyone has worked hard," Maria said.

"We all want Augustania to be perfect," Melody added.

"Why can't everyone just celebrate the way they want?" Andrew asked.

No matter what Elizabeth had said, I could not let everybody else have their own way. "Because I am the one who thought of Augustania!" I blurted out. My friends grew very quiet.

"Karen, you do not have to be such a bossy bragger," Hannie said. She looked me straight in the eye.

I guess I was being bossy. I was right back where I had started. And Elizabeth was right. Being the head of a group was not easy at all. I did not know what to do next.

Just then, Elizabeth yelled, "Karen! There is a telephone call for you."

I ran into the kitchen to answer the phone.

"Hello, Karen," a woman said. "My name is Cami Warner. I am the producer at the

WJSN News Station here in Stoneybrook."

A television producer. How gigundoly cool!

Cami explained that she had heard about the Augustania celebration and wanted to send a crew to film it for the nightly news. I could not believe it! We were going to be on television! Congresswoman Kesser had probably called the TV station. She must have really liked the idea of an August holiday. She was probably meeting with the President right now. I guess that is why she had not called me yet. Augustania *was* going to be a national holiday! Now everyone was going to know about Augustania.

I told Cami about our celebration, and then ran back outside.

"We did it!" I yelled. "Augustania is going to be a real national holiday!"

Everyone cheered and jumped up and down. Then we all chanted, "The sun is hot and the sky is blue. Happy Augustania to you!"

"Now everyone can celebrate Augustania," I said. I looked around at my friends. "Thank you for all your hard work. Augustania is going to be great."

Hannie smiled at me. "Happy Augustania, Karen," she said.

"Happy Augustania," I replied. Then I added, "We made a holiday."

One More Day

"One more day until Augustania," I announced. Andrew and I were with Daddy in his garden. We were helping him water the giant sunflowers. I could not wait to give the flowers to my friends for Augustania.

I love to help Daddy take care of the garden. I especially like to help with the watering. Daddy wheels out the big green hose from the shed, and Andrew and I get to take turns spraying the giant flowers. We have to

be very careful. Daddy likes to take good care of his garden.

"Karen, why don't you and Andrew see if the cookies are ready?" Daddy said when we were done watering.

Nannie had made sunflower cookies for Augustania. And now Andrew, David Michael, and I were going to decorate them with yellow and black sprinkles.

The counters in the kitchen were covered with plates of cookies. We had a lot of work to do. Elizabeth said we should make an assembly line. First Nannie and Kristy frosted the cookies. Then Andrew and I sprinkled the black sprinkles in the middles of the flowers. Then Elizabeth and David Michael used yellow sprinkles for the petals. We were an excellent assembly line. Even Emily Michelle helped out. (But I think she liked eating the sprinkles much more than putting them on the cookies.) Soon we had decorated all the cookie flowers.

"Wow, those are great!" Charlie said

when he saw them. He had been at the beach all day with his friends. Sam came into the kitchen after him. He started to grab a cookie, but Elizabeth said he had to wait until Augustania to have one.

"So Karen's holiday is going to happen?" Sam asked. "Is she going to run for mayor too?"

"Very funny," I said. (I told you big brothers are sometimes a pain.)

"Sam, maybe you should sign up for the pie-eating contest," Kristy said.

Sam loves to eat. "A pie-eating contest?" he asked.

"You can make your own sundae too!" Andrew said.

Suddenly Sam was much more interested in Augustania.

I smiled as I looked at the sunflower cookies. I thought about a yellow shirt and yellow shorts that I could wear. I couldn't wait to hand out my cookies and sunflowers to my family and friends. I also could not wait to swim, make sundaes, and even march in the Dog Days of Summer Parade!

That night I had trouble falling asleep. I snuggled with Moosie and tried to close my eyes, but I was much too excited. I didn't think morning would ever come . . . and I could not wait to start the Augustania celebrations!

Happy Augustania!

"Happy Augustania, Karen!"

I opened my eyes and saw Andrew standing by my bed. It was morning. It was Augustania!

I jumped out of bed. Already the sun was shining and the sky was bright blue. It was a perfect day for a new holiday.

Andrew and I ran downstairs. Daddy, Elizabeth, Nannie, and Emily Michelle were already eating breakfast.

"Happy Augustania!" I said.

I saw four presents on the table. One had

my name on it, one had Andrew's, one had Emily's, and one had David Michael's. Goody, goody, goody!

David Michael ran into the kitchen next. "Happy Augustania, everyone!" he said.

My gift was wrapped in sunflower paper. Inside was a bright yellow shirt with a sunflower on it. Perfect for Augustania.

"Thank you," I said to Daddy and Elizabeth.

Andrew got a new pail and shovel for the beach. He loved them.

Emily's present was a bright yellow bathing suit.

David Michael got a new soccer shirt.

Then Nannie gave us each a giant chocolate sunflower lollipop that she had made herself. They looked too good to eat . . . almost. So far Augustania was great.

After breakfast, Daddy and I went out to Daddy's garden. He cut a bunch of the sunflowers down so I could give them to my friends. They were taller than I was.

When Kristy, Sam, and Charlie woke up, I gave them each a flower and an ice-cream card that I had made. I think that they liked them. They each gave Andrew, David Michael, and me coupons for ice cream at Sullivan Sweets, a yummy store with lots of ice cream and candy.

Elizabeth and Daddy helped David Michael, Andrew, and me get ready for the make-your-own sundaes. We made hot fudge and put out bowls of sprinkles and candies. (We would not put out the ice cream until later.)

"Happy Augustania, Karen!" Hannie and Nancy were at my door. They were dressed all in yellow. Hannie had new sunflower barrettes in her hair and Nancy was wearing a sun pin on her shirt. We all showed one another our gifts.

Kristy said she would walk up and down the street with us to get some candy. Our neighbors gave us lots of treats.

We saw Maria getting ready for the dog

parade. Astrid was wearing a yellow ribbon around her neck.

"Look how cute she is!" Hannie said. It was time for her to get Noodle ready too.

I saw Timmy and Scott with their aviator sunglasses. Their dog, Clyde, was happy to be part of the parade.

"Are you Karen Brewer?" A woman tapped me on the shoulder. A microphone was in her hand.

"Yes," I answered. I knew right away that she was Cami Warner from WJSN.

I took Cami and her crew to the Kormans' house, where the luau swim party had begun. Bill and Maria were teaching everyone a Hawaiian dance.

Later, we went to the Hsus', where the pie-eating contest was going on. It was a close race between Linny and Sam. Finally Sam won.

The last stop was my house, for the make-your-own sundaes. I think the cameraman really liked that stop. He ate two sundaes.

"Karen, what do you think of today?" Cami asked.

I looked right into the camera. "This is the best holiday ever," I said. "Happy Augustania to everyone!"

Bad News, Good News

After the television crew left, everyone started to clean up and go back to their own houses. I helped Elizabeth clean up the kitchen. There were lots of dirty ice-cream bowls from the sundaes.

"Where is today's mail?" Charlie asked Elizabeth.

"I think it is on the table in the hallway," she said.

"Look, here is something for you, Karen," Charlie said as he handed me an envelope.

I looked at the letter. It was from Congresswoman Kesser!

I opened the envelope. The letter said that a national holiday takes years to happen. It needs to be discussed by the Congress and the Senate. Boo and bullfrogs.

"Who is the letter from?" Elizabeth asked.

I handed it to Elizabeth. "Why did the television crew come to film Augustania if it is not a national holiday?" I said.

Elizabeth put down the letter and led me to the couch in the living room. She sat down and asked me to sit down next to her.

"Karen, I told my friend at WJSN about Augustania," Elizabeth explained. "You and your friends worked so hard that I thought people should know about your holiday celebration."

"So Augustania is not a national holiday?" I asked.

"No, Karen," Elizabeth said. She gave me a tight hug. "I'm sorry if that is what you thought. But Augustania was a real holiday for you and your friends."

Daddy poked his head into the living room. "Karen, why don't you invite your friends over for a barbecue tonight, and then you can watch yourselves on the news."

That sounded like a great idea. I called my friends and everyone came over for dinner. (But Sam and Linny did not feel like eating too much after all that pie.)

At seven o'clock, we sat down in front of the television set.

"Look, there is Cami Warner!" Nancy said.

We watched Cami walking down our street. She explained to the viewers about Augustania. She even mentioned all of our names. Then we saw ourselves at the dog parade, the luau, the pie-eating contest, and in the big-house kitchen making sundaes.

I was happy to be on television and to see

my friends. But I was still sad that Augustania was not going to be a national holiday.

Just when the news program was ending,
the phone rang. Kristy said that it was for
me. And that is when my bad news turned
into good news.

Augustania Forever!

"Hello? This is Karen Brewer," I said into the phone.

"Hello, my name is Stephen Andrews," a boy said. "I'm from Farmington."

It was the boy from *Kid Power!*, one of the organizers of the big playground cleanup.

He told me he had just seen the report on television about Augustania. He said he really liked the dog parade, the sunflowers, and all the ice cream.

"Augustania was a great idea," he said.

"Thanks," I replied. "It was a lot of work.

It was hard to be a leader of an important committee. But my friends and I had a great time."

"My friends and I are looking for a new project," Stephen said. "Would you mind if we had an Augustania celebration of our own?"

Wow! How gigundoly cool! I was about to give him my answer, but then I remembered my friends. I knew that as a good committee head, I had to ask them what they thought. After all, it was not just up to me. It was up to all the founders of Augustania. I asked Stephen to hang on for a minute.

I ran into the den and told my friends about the phone call.

"Cool!" Hannie and Maria said.

"He saw us on TV?" Nancy said, giggling. "We are famous!"

"All right, Augustania!" David Michael said as he hit a high five with Linny.

"So what do you think?" I asked. "Should we tell Stephen it is all right?"

"*Yessss!*" everyone answered.

I ran back to the phone. I told Stephen that he should definitely celebrate Augustania in Farmington! He wanted to know how we planned the day and everything about our committees.

When I hung up the phone, I went back to my friends. They were eating watermelon and talking about the day. Daddy had taped the news program, so we watched the video of our holiday all over again. It was fun to see my friends on television. I especially liked the end, when Cami Warner interviewed me!

"Wow, we did it, Karen," Hannie said.

"We all worked together," Melody added.

"Three cheers for Augustania!" I shouted.

"Hip, hip, hooray! Hip, hip, hooray! Hip, hip, hooray!" we cheered.

Maybe Augustania was not a real national holiday, but it was going to be celebrated in another town. Maybe it would even be celebrated across the whole state. Long live Augustania!

L. GODWIN

About the Author

ANN M. MARTIN lives in New York City and loves animals, especially cats. She has two cats of her own, Gussie and Woody.

Other books by Ann M. Martin that you might enjoy are *Stage Fright*; *Me and Katie (the Pest)*; and the books in *The Baby-sitters Club* series.

Ann likes ice cream and *I Love Lucy*. And she has her own little sister, whose name is Jane.

BABY-SITTERS
Little Sister

Don't miss #113

KAREN'S HURRICANE

"Attention, attention, please, all classes," came Mrs. Titus's voice. "An actual hurricane warning, not a watch, has been issued for a wide area of Connecticut, including Stoneybrook and the surrounding towns."

I gasped and turned to look at Hannie and Nancy. Their eyes were big and round.

"Classes are being dismissed for the day, so that students and teachers can get home safely and prepare for the hurricane," said Mrs. Titus.

I put my hand over my mouth. Oh my goodness! Hurricane Karen was heading straight for Stoneybrook!